"My favorite is the Tilt-A-Whirl. It spins so fast you can barely hold your head up!" Junior was dizzy at the very thought of it.

"The Ferris wheel," Maddie answered quickly. "You can see the whole county from the top!"

As they waited in the line of traffic, Junior's mom reminded them of the rules, "Okay, kids, meet us at the front gate at four-thirty. And please don't spend all of your money on those silly carnival games."

Junior's dad stopped at the front gate, and Junior and his friends exploded out of the car.

"Stick together and remember the rules!" Mom called.

"Okay, Mom!" Junior called back.

"Follow me!"
Maddie ran toward the rides.

"First stop, the Tilt-A-Whirl!"
Junior answered.

But after a few minutes, Junior
turned back to see that Billy
had stopped running.

"Look! The Balloon Race!" Billy called.
Junior and Maddie ran back toward him.
"Let's play this! Then, next stop:
the Tilt-A-Whirl."

"Well, I do have money in my
Game envelope." Junior pulled three
envelopes out of his pocket.

"Games. Rides. Food." Maddie read them aloud. "From *Dollar Bill's Adventures*?"

Junior nodded. "Yep, I budgeted my spending money into the three things I wanted to do tonight. That way, I won't spend it all in one place."

"Ooookay," the man said in his announcer voice, "when the bell rings, shoot the water into the clown's mouth to fill the balloon! The first one to pop the balloon is the winner!"

Junior closed one eye, the bell rang, and each stream of water hit the clown right in the mouth. Junior focused only on that clown's mouth until . . .

POP!

"YES! I won!" Billy shouted. His gaze turned to the big, blue teddy bear.

"Here ya go, kid." The man handed him a plastic duck keychain. "Win five of these and you can trade in for the pink puppy."

"But—but what about the blue bear?"

The man laughed. "Son, you'll need three pink puppies to trade in for that."

"Oooo, Skee-Ball!" Junior shouted. "We can all play, put our tickets together, and get a really big prize!"

"Yeah!" Maddie agreed.

Billy looked at his keychain. "Sure."

Junior slung those wooden balls up the ramp until his Game envelope was empty. "I'm out," he told the other two.

"That row?"
Billy asked.
The lady nodded.

Junior picked a
loopy straw, Maddie
chose a plastic ring,
and Billy got another
duck keychain.

And there in front of them all was a huge, black-and-white Dalmatian with a big red bow.

"That . . . is the biggest and cutest Dalmatian . . . I have ever seen," Maddie said, almost robotically.

"Oh no." Junior just shook his head.

"Come on, guys! I know one of us can win," pleaded Maddie.

"Okay." Junior sighed. "But just one more game."

They all ran to the counter, and Maddie handed the man a dollar for three darts. She planted her feet and focused on the balloons. The first dart sailed through the air and POP went the first balloon. She threw the second dart. POP!

"Oh, I'm so close to getting the Dalmatian!" Maddie exclaimed. She took a deep breath and released the dart.

BONK!

The dart bounced off of the board and landed on the ground.

"No!" she cried.

"I'll try!" Junior and Billy both said in unison.

All three kids stood at the counter with their darts. They all popped two balloons, but no one could get the third balloon.

They tried and tried, and, before they knew, they had used all of their Food money. Then they began using their Ride money. They played dollar after dollar after dollar.

Junior handed his last dollar to the game man. He bit his bottom lip, squinted his eyes, and threw the first dart. **BONK!** He missed.

"Sorry, kids! Better luck next time," said the game man.

As Junior, Maddie, and Billy circled back to the front gate, they passed the Tilt-A-Whirl. Junior watched the riders spinning so fast and laughing so loudly. He looked through his three empty envelopes one last time. "Maybe next year," he sighed.

"Hey, kids! Did you have a great time?"
Dad asked as they climbed into the car.

"Yeah."

"Sure."

"Mm-hmm."

Mom and Dad looked at each other. "You didn't spend all your money on those carnival games, did you?" Mom asked. But she already knew the answer.

After Dad had taken home Billy and Maddie, he looked back at Junior in the rearview mirror. "So, what happened, bud?"

"The envelopes didn't work," Junior said flatly. "I had it all planned out, but then Maddie wanted this Dalmatian so much, Dad. I *had* to help her win it."

"Did she win it?"

Junior shook his head. "I should have just stuck to the plan."

"I think you're right," Dad answered.
"Those envelopes can't do it all by themselves."

The next Saturday, Mom pulled up beside a Yard Sale sign, and Junior jumped out of the van. "How much is the radio?" a breathless Junior asked the man in the lawn chair.

"Ten dollars," he answered.

Junior pulled out his envelope and counted.
"Five, six, seven." For a split second, he thought about that other envelope in his back pocket, but then shook his head. "Thanks, Mister," he said and walked over to another table.

And there it was—a huge, black-and-white Dalmatian with a big, red bow. And the sticker said one dollar.

"Junior!" Maddie gasped when she opened the door. "Where did you find him?"

Junior smiled. "Bought him."

"Wait." Maddie put a hand on her hip. "You didn't spend all your envelopes again, did you?"

"No way! I've learned my lesson there," Junior answered. "The only way the envelopes work is to make them work for you."

"Dollar Bill would
be proud," she said.
And with that, she
gave her Dalmatian
a great, big hug.

DEDICATION

Rachel is my middle child, the one who learned these principles as we lived them!

She has been our barometer to make sure we're teaching the kids well.

And, in fact, she was the inspiration for this story!

Thank you, Rachel, for being wide-eyed and desiring to experience life to the fullest while continuing to gain wisdom from your mom and dad.

Love, Dad (Dave)

"This is going to be awesome!" Junior beamed with excitement as he sat in the backseat between his best friends Billy and Maddie.

"What should we ride first?" Billy asked.

CARELESS AT THE CARNIVAL
Junior Discovers Spending

by **Dave Ramsey**

Collect all of the *Junior's Adventures* books!

For more information on Dave Ramsey, visit daveramsey.com or call 888.227.3223.

Editors: Amy Parker, Jen Gingerich
Project Management: Preston Cannon, Bryan Amerine and Mallory Darcy
Illustrations: Greg Hardin, John Trent and Kenny Yamada
Art Direction: Luke LeFevre, Brad Dennison and Chris Carrico